PROFESSOR VON VOLT IS A FAMOUS SCIENTIST. HE DESIGNED THIS TIME MACHINE FOR THE STILTON FAMILY: THEIR MISSION IS TO DEFEAT THE PIRATE CATS AND SAVE HISTORY!

SPEEDRAT

Geronimo Stilton

THE COLISEUM CON

PAPERCUTZ™

Geronimo Stilton

GRAPHIC NOVELS AVAILABLE FROM PAPERCUTZ

#1
"The Discovery of America"

#2
"The Secret of the Sphinx"

#3
"The Coliseum Con"

#4
"Following the Trail of Marco Polo"

#5
"The Great Ice Age"

#6
"Who Stole The Mona Lisa?"

#7
"Dinosaurs in Action"

#8
"Play It Again, Mozart!"

#9
"The Weird Book Machine"

#10
"Geronimo Stilton Saves the Olympics"

#11
"We'll Always Have Paris"

#12
"The First Samurai"

#13
"The Fastest Train in the West"

#14
"The First Mouse on the Moon"

#15
"All for Stilton, Stilton for All!"

#16
"Lights, Camera, Stilton!"

#17
"The Mystery of the Pirate Ship"

#18
"First to the Last Place on Earth"

#19
"Lost in Translation"

GERONIMO STILTON REPORTER #1
"Operation ShuFongfong"

GERONIMO STILTON REPORTER #2
"It's My Scoop"
COMING SOON

GERONIMO STILTON REPORTER #3
"Stop Acting Around"
COMING SOON

GERONIMO STILTON 3 in 1 #1

GERONIMO STILTON 3 in 1 #2

GERONIMO STILTON 3 in 1 #3
COMING SOON

...ALSO AVAILABLE WHEREVER E-BOOKS ARE SOLD!

papercutz.com

Geronimo Stilton

THE COLISEUM CON
By Geronimo Stilton

PAPERCUT Z™
New York

THE COLISEUM CON
© EDIZIONI PIEMME 2007 S.p.A.
Via Tiziano 32, 20145
Milan, Italy

Text by Geronimo Stilton
Based on an original idea by Elisabetta Dami.
Editorial coordination by Patrizia Puricelli in collaboration with Tommaso Valsecchi
Original editing by Daniela Finistauri
Script by Demetrio Bargellini
Artistic coordination by Roberta Bianchi
Artistic assistance by Tommaso Valsecchi
Graphic Project by Michela Battaglin
Graphics by Marta Lorini
Cover art and color by Flavio Ferron
Interior illustrations and color by Ambrogio M. Piazzoni

© 2009 – for this work in English language by Papercutz.

Original title: Geronimo Stilton La Truffa Del Colosseo

Translation by: Nanette McGuinness

www.geronimostilton.com

Lettering and Production by Ortho
Michael Petranek – Associate Editor
Jim Salicrup
Editor-in-Chief

ISBN: 978-1-59707-172-7

Printed in India
July 2022

Distributed by Macmillan.
Fifteenth Papercutz Printing

IT WAS A BEAUTIFUL MORNING IN NEW MOUSE CITY. A WARM BREEZE WAS BLOWING, GIVING THE CITY A TASTE OF SPRING.

THE COLISEUM CON

BUT THAT VERY MORNING, MY ALARM CLOCK DIDN'T GO OFF AND I WAS *VERY* LATE!

OH, EXCUSE ME, I HAVEN'T INTRODUCED MYSELF YET. MY NAME IS STILTON, GERONIMO STILTON, AND I EDIT THE RODENT'S GAZETTE, THE MOST FAMOUSE PAPER ON MOUSE ISLAND.

SO AS I WAS SAYING, I WAS *RUNNING* WHEN...

->PUFF! PUFF!<-

SLAM

->SQUEAK!<-

5

—:SQUEAK!:—
MY POOR TAIL!

—:SQUEEAK!:—
MY POOR PAW!

—:SQUEEEAK!:—
MY POOR NOSE!

BAM

OOPS!

I FINALLY GOT TO THE OFFICE, BUT MY TROUBLES WEREN'T OVER...

GERONIMO, THERE'S A VERY IMPORTANT VISITOR FOR YOU!

IT WAS THE FAMOUS OPERA SINGER RATIDO DOMINGO!

AH, GOOD MORNING, DR. STILTON!

UM... GOOD MORNING!

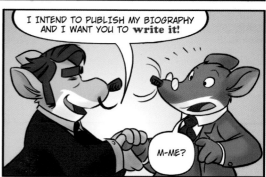

I INTEND TO PUBLISH MY BIOGRAPHY AND I WANT YOU TO **write it!**

M-ME?

I GREATLY ADMIRE YOUR BOOKS AND I KNOW YOU'LL BE ABLE TO FIND THE RIGHT WORDS TO DESCRIBE MY ART! LISTEN...

BE GONE, OH RAT! FADE AWAY, MOZZARELLA! AT DAWN, I SHALL SQUEAK...!

?!?

I GOT RID OF RATIDO BY PROMISING TO THINK ABOUT HIS IDEA AND STARTED WORKING, BUT I WAS IMMEDIATELY INTERRUPTED...

IT WAS MY GRANDFATHER, WILLIAM SHORTPAWS, NICKNAMED "TANK"...

UM...HELLO, GRANDPA!

WAKE UP!

HAVE YOU READ THE THE DAILY RAT?

ACTUALLY, THAT'S SALLY RATMOUSEN'S PAPER. MINE'S CALLED...

I KNOW PERFECTLY WELL WHAT THE PAPER I FOUNDED IS CALLED!

THAT RAT'S PAPER HAS AN ARTICLE ON RATIDO DOMINGO'S CONCERT, BUT THERE'S NOTHING ABOUT IT IN THE RODENT GAZETTE!

RATIDO? THAT'S ODD... HE WAS HERE A LITTLE WHILE AGO!

WHAT? AND YOU DIDN'T INTERVIEW HIM?

WHAT DO YOU DO IN YOUR OFFICE, SLEEP? WAKE UUUP!!!

WAKE UP!

WAKE UP!

?!?

?!?

WAKE UUUUP!!!!

CRASH

CRASH

CRASH

GRANDSON? ARE YOU STILL THERE? WHAT ARE YOU DOING... ARE YOU REALLY ASLEEP?

AFTER A DAY LIKE THAT, I DIDN'T WANT TO DO ANYTHING BESIDES GO HOME AND NIBBLE ON SOME CRACKERS AND CHEESE...

INSTEAD...

ROTTEN ROQUEFORT! THE REFRIGERATOR'S EMPTY!

~SIGH!~

DEAR COUSIN, I WAS PASSING THROUGH AND GOT HUNGRY! NEXT TIME COULD YOU BUY SOME FRESH MOZZARELLA, TOO? THANKS! TRAP

I WAS ABOUT TO GO LOOK FOR A STORE THAT WAS OPEN, WHEN...

MY CELL PHONE?

RRINGGRRINGG

WHO KNOWS WHO THAT IS? LET'S HOPE IT'S NOT SOMEONE ELSE WHO WANTS TO SCREAM IN MY EAR!

RRINGGRRINGG

H-HELLO?

HELLO, GERONIMO? IT'S AMPY VON VOLT!

AH, GOOD EVENING, PROFESSOR!

SORRY TO DISTURB YOU, BUT YOU MUST COME TO MY LABORATORY RIGHT AWAY!

NOW? TO TELL THE TRUTH, I...

IT'S AN EMERGENCY! THE PIRATE CATS HAVE GONE INTO ACTION!

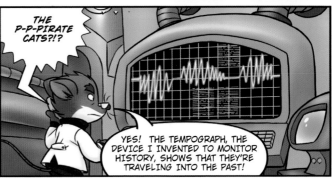

THE P-P-PIRATE CATS?!?

YES! THE TEMPOGRAPH, THE DEVICE I INVENTED TO MONITOR HISTORY, SHOWS THAT THEY'RE TRAVELING INTO THE PAST!

9

OKAY, PROFESSOR... I'M COMING! WHERE'S YOUR LAB TODAY?

NEARBY! YOU JUST HAVE TO GO DOWN TO THE BASEMENT...I'VE TAKEN CARE OF THE REST!

MY BASEMENT?

YES, AND ONCE YOU'RE IN THE BASE-MENT...

YOU'LL SEE AN ENORMOUS WHEEL OF CHEESE UP AGAINST THE WALL! BEHIND IT THERE'S A SECRET PASSAGE!

?

MOVE THE CHEESE, CRAWL INTO THE HOLE...

...AND HAVE A NICE TRIP!

WATCH OUT FOR JOLTS!

?!?

10

FSSHOOOMM

WUMP!

GERONIMO, ARE YOU OKAY?

~GLUB!~ WHERE AM I?

SORRY ABOUT THE TRIP, BUT CONNECTING YOUR BASEMENT TO MY LABORATORY WAS THE QUICKEST WAY TO GET YOU HERE!

Y-YES, OF COURSE, I UNDERSTAND...

Uncle Geronimo!

BENJAMIN! YOU'RE HERE, TOO?

AND THAT'S ALSO WHY WE'RE HERE!

CIAO, UNCLE G!

THEA! BUGSY WUGSY! THE PROFESSOR CALLED YOU TOO!

I'LL NEED ALL OF YOUR HELP TO FOIL THE PIRATE CATS' PLAN!

DID YOU TAKE A RIDE ON THAT HORRIBLE SLIDE TOO?

NO, YOU'RE THE ONLY LUCKY ONE! THE KIDS AND I WERE "SATISFIED" WITH THE SUBWAY.

AND WHERE'S TRAP?

HE DIDN'T COME. I TRIED TO CALL HIM, BUT I COULDN'T FIND HIM...

MEANWHILE...

OOF... I WAS HOPING GERONIMO'D GONE SHOPPING AGAIN!

TELL US, PROFESSOR, WHAT'S THE PIRATE CATS' DESTINATION THIS TIME AROUND?

THE TEMPOGRAPH SHOWS THAT THEY'RE HEADING TO *ANCIENT ROME*, IN THE YEAR 80 A.D., DURING THE REIGN OF EMPEROR TITUS.

ROME

ROME

ACCORDING TO THE LEGEND, THE CITY OF ROME WAS FOUNDED IN AROUND 753 B.C. BY ROMULUS, THE FIRST OF SEVEN KINGS (THE OTHERS WERE, IN ORDER: NUMA POMPILIUS, TULLUS HOSTILLIUS, ANCUS MARCIUS, L. TARQUINIUS PRISCUS, SERVIUS TULLIUS AND TARQUINIUS SUPERBUS). WHEN IT BECAME A REPUBLIC, ROME EXTENDED ITS RULE ACROSS THE ENTIRE BASIN OF THE MEDITERRANEAN SEA AND BECAME THE GREATEST POWER OF THE TIME. AFTER A PERIOD OF CIVIL WAR, GAIUS JULIUS CAESAR OCTAVIUS, CAESAR'S NEPHEW, TOOK POWER, TRANSFORMED THE REPUBLIC INTO AN EMPIRE, AND HAD HIMSELF NAMED AUGUSTUS. THE OFFICIAL LANGUAGE OF ANCIENT ROME WAS LATIN, BUT GREEK WAS ALSO SPOKEN WIDELY.

FANTASTIC! I'VE ALWAYS DREAMED OF VISITING ANCIENT ROME!

DO YOU HAVE AN IDEA WHY THEY CHOSE THAT YEAR?

WELL, THE ONLY EVENT WORTH MENTIONING...

...IS THE INAUGURATION OF THE FLAVIAN AMPHITHEATER, BETTER KNOWN AS THE COLISEUM!

THE FLAVIAN AMPHITHEATER (BETTER KNOWN AS THE COLISEUM)

BEGUN IN AROUND 72 A.D. BY EMPEROR VESPASIAN, THE AMPHITHEATER WAS FINISHED AND INAUGURATED IN AROUND 80 A.D., UNDER EMPEROR TITUS. THE AMPHITHEATER WAS GIVEN THE NAME FLAVIAN IN HONOR OF VESPASIAN AND TITUS, WHO BELONGED TO THE FLAVIAN "GENS" (THAT'S "FAMILY" IN LATIN). THE DERIVATION OF THE NAME "COLISEUM" -- WHICH THE AMPHITHEATER HAS COME TO BE KNOWN BY THROUGHOUT THE WORLD -- IS LESS CERTAIN. ACCORDING TO SOME STORIES, THE NAME COMES FROM THE FACT THAT IN ANCIENT TIMES, A GIGANTIC STATUE OF THE EMPEROR NERO NAMED THE "COLOSSUS NERONIS," -- THAT'S THE "COLOSSUS OF NERO" -- LOOMED NEARBY. MORE THAN 150 FEET TALL AND WITH THREE ROWS OF ARCHES, THE COLISEUM COULD HOLD 50,000 SPECTATORS. INSIDE, THE SO-CALLED "ROMAN CIRCUS" WAS HELD, WHICH HAD GAMES AND ALSO GLADIATORIAL COMBAT -- EVEN SHIP BATTLES (THE AMPHITHEATER WAS FILLED WITH WATER SOMETIMES). IN THE UPPER PART OF THE AMPHITHEATER, THERE WERE WOODEN POLES FOR HOLDING UP CANVAS TENTS, WHICH WERE TO PROTECT SPECTATORS FROM THE SUN. UNDER THE CENTRAL PART OF THE AMPHITHEATER THERE WERE ROOMS AND SUBTERRANEAN CORRIDORS, IN WHICH THE MEN, ANIMALS, AND MACHINERY FOR THE GAMES WERE HIDDEN.

THE COLISEUM? WHAT COULD THE PIRATE CATS DO WITH IT?

MAYBE THEY WANT TO TURN IT INTO A MARBLE URN... HEE HEE HEE!

?!!?

A-A-AM I WRONG OR DID THAT GIFT BOX JUST SP-SP-SPEAK?

SPEAKING OF WHICH... THAT PACKAGE ARRIVED AT THE OFFICE FOR YOU AND I THOUGHT I'D BRING IT HERE.

COULD A SPY FOR THE PIRATE CATS BE HIDING INSIDE IT?

—GULP!— A SPY...IN MY SECRET LABORATORY!

COME ON, GERONIMO! OPEN IT!

M-ME?

SQUEAK-A-BOO?✳

AHHH!

✳SURPRISE!

13

HEY, STILTON-BABY! DID YOU LIKE MY LITTLE JOKE?

HERCULE POIRAT?!?

→MMF! MMF!←

THANK GOODNESS, IT'S YOUR DETECTIVE FRIEND!

HEE, HEE, HEE... HE ADORES PLAYING TRICKS ON PEOPLE!

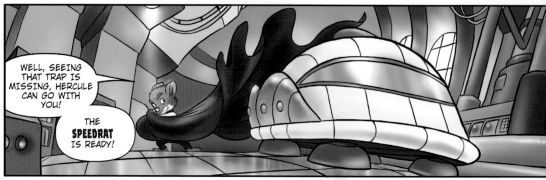

WELL, SEEING THAT TRAP IS MISSING, HERCULE CAN GO WITH YOU!

THE **SPEEDRAT** IS READY!

BILLIONS OF BUNCHES OF BANANAS! IS THAT VON VOLT'S TIME MACHINE?

EXACTLY! ARE YOU COMING WITH US?

DO YOU THINK THEA WILL AGREE?

YOU'LL HAVE TO ASK HER...

SO! HAVE YOU TWO DECIDED TO GET ON BOARD?

I'M YOURS TO COMMAND, THEA!

HE'S REALLY IN LOVE!

SO...

I PUT ANCIENT ROMAN *CLO*THING UNDER THE SEATS...

AND SOME *SESTERCES!*

SESTERCES

IN ANCIENT ROME THERE WERE VARIOUS DIFFERENT COINS: THE AS, SESTERCE (WHICH WAS WORTH ABOUT TWO AND A HALF AS), DENARIUS (WORTH ABOUT FOUR SESTERCES) AND AUREUS (WORTH ABOUT 25 DENARI). EACH EMPEROR HAD HIS OWN IMAGE AND HIS MOST SIGNIFICANT ACCOMPLISHMENTS DEPICTED ON THEM.

14

MY SPECIAL EARPHONES FOR SPEAKING AND UNDERSTANDING THE LANGUAGE OF THE TIME ARE ON THE DASHBOARD.

THANKS! YOU'LL SEE: WE'LL STOP THE CATS!

YES! WE'LL SAVE HISTORY!

TAKE OFF!

ZZZzKKKRRAAKKK

ZZZZZOOOMM

LET'S HOPE THEY SUCCEED AGAIN THIS TIME...

FSSHOOOMM

WHAT'S GOING ON?

?!?

TRAP? HOW COME YOU'RE HERE?

WHY AM I HERE? I REMEMBER I WAS LOOKING FOR SOME FOOD IN GERONIMO'S BASEMENT AND I CRAWLED INTO A HOLE IN THE WALL...

SPEAKING OF SNACKS... YOU WOULDN'T HAVE SOMETHING TO MUNCH ON, WOULD YOU?

...

IN THE MEANTIME, OTHERS HAVE ALREADY ARRIVED IN ANCIENT ROME...

STEADY AS SHE GOES, BONZO! FOLLOW THE TIBER!

BUT WHERE, TERSILLA? I CAN'T SEE ANYTHING IN THIS MIST!

VRRRRR

THE TIBER

IS A RIVER IN CENTRAL ITALY. IT ORIGINATES ON MT. FUMAIOLO, WHICH IS IN THE APENNINES IN EMILIA-ROMAGNA, AND CROSSES THROUGH THE CITY OF ROME, CONTINUING THEN TO FLOW INTO THE TYRRHENIAN SEA. IT'S ABOUT 400 KILOMETERS LONG. DURING THE TIME OF ANCIENT ROME, THE TIBER WAS A MAJOR ROUTE FOR COMMUNICATION, USED TO TRANSPORT MANY GOODS FROM THE SEA TO ROME, AND CONTINUING INLAND FROM THERE.

SO USE THE RADAR! JUST MAKE SURE YOU DON'T SLAM INTO THE RIVER BANK.

OKAY, OKAY! BUT I DON'T UNDERSTAND WHY IT'S ALWAYS MY TURN TO DRIVE!

BECAUSE I'M CATARDONE, RULER OF THE PIRATE CATS AND SHE'S MY DAUGHTER! DON'T YOU HAVE ANYTHING BETWEEN YOUR EARS?

OW! THAT BLOW'S BETWEEN MY EARS... BUT NOT THE EXPLANATION!

16

MEOW DOWN*, DADDY DEAR! HERE'S THE CLOACA MAXIMA, ANCIENT ROME'S SEWER SYSTEM! LET'S HIDE THE CATJET HERE!

BLECH, IN THE SEWER? THAT DOESN'T SEEM VERY DIGNIFIED FOR A KING!

QUIET, YOU HAIRBALL

*CALM DOWN

THE CLOACA MAXIMA

ROME IS THE MOST ANCIENT CITY TO HAVE BUILT A NETWORK OF SEWERS FOR DUMPING LIQUID REFUSE. CONSTRUCTED IN THE 6TH CENTURY B.C. BY THE LAST KINGS OF ROME, THE CLOACA MAXIMA WAS DUG OUT BELOW GROUND LEVEL. ORIGINALLY IT WAS AN OPEN-AIR CANAL THAT LIQUID REFUSE WAS THROWN INTO. ONLY LATER WAS IT COVERED OVER.

PULL OVER, BONZO!

TERSILLA, WHY ARE WE IN ANCIENT ROME?

WHAT A STENCH!

SIMPLE, DADDY DEAR...WE'RE GOING TO SEIZE THE COLISEUM!

THE COLISEUM? AND WHAT ARE WE GOING TO DO WITH THE COLISEUM?

MAKE IT INTO A MARBLE RUN!

WOULDN'T YOU LIKE IT IF THEY NAMED THE AMPHITHEATER "CATAR-DONIUS?"

HMM... ACTUALLY, THAT SOUNDS NICE!

YES... FOR A MARBLE RUN!

IF THE COLISEUM HAD YOUR NAME, THE PIRATE CAT LINEAGE WOULD BE FAMOUS THROUGHOUT THE CENTURIES!

THROUGHOUT THE CENTURIES... AND IN MARBLE MANUALS!

CUT IT OUT WITH THE MARBLE STORY!

~GULP!~

GO ON! I IMAGINE YOU'VE ALREADY THOUGHT OF A PLAN...

YES, DADDY, I'VE THOUGHT OF EVERYTHING! I'LL TELL YOU THE DETAILS ON THE WAY!

AH, IF IT WEREN'T FOR ME!

COME ON, LET'S PUT ON OUR MOUSE MASKS AND DISGUISE OURSELVES AS ANCIENT ROMANS!

A FEW MINUTES LATER...

PERFECT! DRESSED LIKE THIS, WE CAN MOVE AROUND UNDISTURBED!

WAIT A MINUTE.... WHY ARE YOUR TUNICS ELEGANT AND MINE ALL RATTY?

BECAUSE CATARDONE AND I ARE GOING TO PRETEND TO BE TWO RICH ROMANS FROM THE PROVINCES AND YOU'RE GOING TO GET HIRED AS A WORKER AT THE COLISEUM!

A WORKER? BUT I DON'T WANT TO WORK!

YOU ARE SUCH A TAIL SMASHER!* STOP IT AND LET'S GET MOVING!

~SIGH!~

*A PAIN

18

SUCH TRAFFIC! I DIDN'T THINK ROME WOULD BE SO CROWDED!

STOP YOUR BELLYACHING, BONZO, WE'RE THERE!

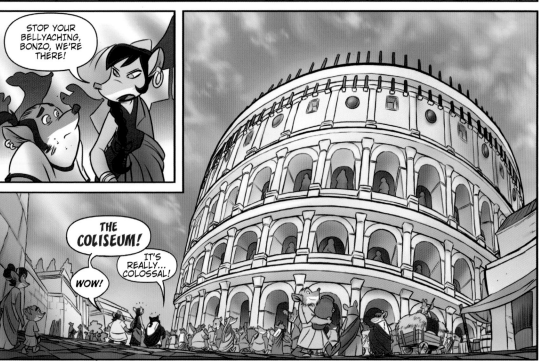

THE COLISEUM!

WOW!

IT'S... REALLY... COLOSSAL!

NOW THAT WE'RE HERE, WHAT ARE WE GOING TO DO?

BONZO WILL GET HIRED AS A WORKER WHILE YOU AND I WILL GO FIND EMPEROR TITUS!

WE'LL SEE THAT WE BECOME HIS FRIENDS AND ATTEND THE INAUGURATION OF THE COLISEUM...

HEE, HEE, HEE... AND THEN WHAT DO YOU HAVE IN MIND, TERSILLA?

I REALLY HAVE TO EXPLAIN EVERYTHING TO YOU, HUH?

UM... NO, I GET WHAT YOUR PLAN IS... BONZO, LET'S SEE IF YOU KNOW IT, TOO!

?

UM, LET'S SEE...DURING THE INAUGURATION, I WILL PRETEND TO ATTACK THE EMPEROR...

...SO CATARDONE WILL BE ABLE TO PRETEND TO SAVE HIM AND THEN, IN REWARD, ASK TITUS TO NAME THE COLISEUM AFTER HIM!

WHAT ARE YOU LOOKING AT ME LIKE THAT FOR, TERSILLA? DID I SAY SOMETHING RATICULOUS*?

*RIDICULOUS

NO, NO, THAT'S REALLY THE PLAN! I'M SURPRISED THAT YOU FIGURED IT OUT YOURSELF!

SO, CAN I BE A RICH ROMAN, TOO?

TRIM YOUR SAILS*, BONZO, YOU HAVE TO BE AT THE COLISEUM AND FIND A JOB WHERE YOU CAN ATTACK TITUS!

*DON'T GET FULL OF YOURSELF

A LITTLE LATER...

NAME AND **ADDRESS.**

CAIUS BONZUS. ADDRESS... CLOACA MAXIMA!

GOOD, BONZO'S BEEN HIRED! WE CAN GO TO THE IMPERIAL PALACE!

EMPEROR TITUS

THE EMPEROR'S FULL NAME WAS TITUS FLAVIUS VESPASIANUS BUT HE CAME TO BE CALLED JUST TITUS IN ORDER TO DISTINGUISH HIM FROM HIS FATHER, WHO HAD THE SAME NAME AND WENT DOWN IN HISTORY AS VESPASIAN. TITUS WAS AN EMPEROR GREATLY LOVED BY HIS PEOPLE. HIS POLICIES WERE INSPIRED BY THE PRINCIPLES OF LEGALITY, GENEROSITY, AND MERCY: DURING HIS ENTIRE REIGN (79 A.D.-81 A.D.) TITUS AVOIDED WIELDING THE DEATH PENALTY, WHICH WAS IN FORCE AT THAT TIME.

STOP! STOP! THERE'S BEEN A MISTAKE!

FORGIVE MY FATHER'S CLUMSINESS! HE DIDN'T MEAN TO DO YOU ANY HARM!

WHO ARE YOU?

MY NAME IS LICINIA MOUSILLA AND HE IS CATARDONIUS CATARDICUS. WE BELONG TO A NOBLE FAMILY THAT LIVES IN ALEXANDRIA IN EGYPT!

IN ALEXANDRIA? THAT CITY IS VERY DEAR TO MY FAMILY... MY FATHER WAS THERE WHEN HE WAS CHOSEN EMPEROR!

OH, I KNOW IT! I KNOW IT VERY WELL!

PRAETORIANS! LET THAT RODENT GO!

AS YOU WISH, EMPEROR!

-PHEW!-

THE PRAETORIANS

THE PRAETORIAN GUARD WAS ORGANIZED BY EMPEROR AUGUSTUS (WHO RULED FROM 27 B.C.–14 A.D.) AND PERMANENTLY FOUNDED BY HIS SUCCESSOR, TIBERIUS (WHO RULED FROM 14 A.D.–37 A.D.). THE PRAETORIANS' PRIMARY TASK WAS TO PROTECT THE EMPEROR, BUT THEY ALSO PERFORMED ADMINISTRATIVE TASKS AND SECRET MISSIONS.

TELL ME, WHAT BRINGS YOU TO ROME?

WE'RE HERE TO SEE THE INAUGURATION OF THE AMPHITHEATER!

YOU UNDERTOOK A VERY LONG AND TIRING JOURNEY. YOUR CURIOSITY DESERVES TO BE REWARDED!

A LITTLE LATER...

THE RUMORS WEREN'T EXAGGERATED AT ALL, DIVINE EMPEROR! SEEN FROM THE INSIDE, THE AMPHITHEATER IS EVEN MORE *EXTRAORDINARY!*

THE CREDIT BELONGS TO HIM: THE ARCHI-TECT, FLAVIANUS RATICUM!

AVE*, TITUS!

*HAIL

YOU ARE VERY GENEROUS! BUT THE PRAISE SHOULD GO TO THE WORKERS!

WITHOUT THEIR SKILL, NOTHING WOULD'VE BEEN POSSI-BLE!

EVEN THE NEW WORK-ERS ARE BEHAVING WELL?

YES! ALL OF THEM, EXCEPT FOR A STRANGE RODENT WHO JUST GOT HERE TODAY!

?!?

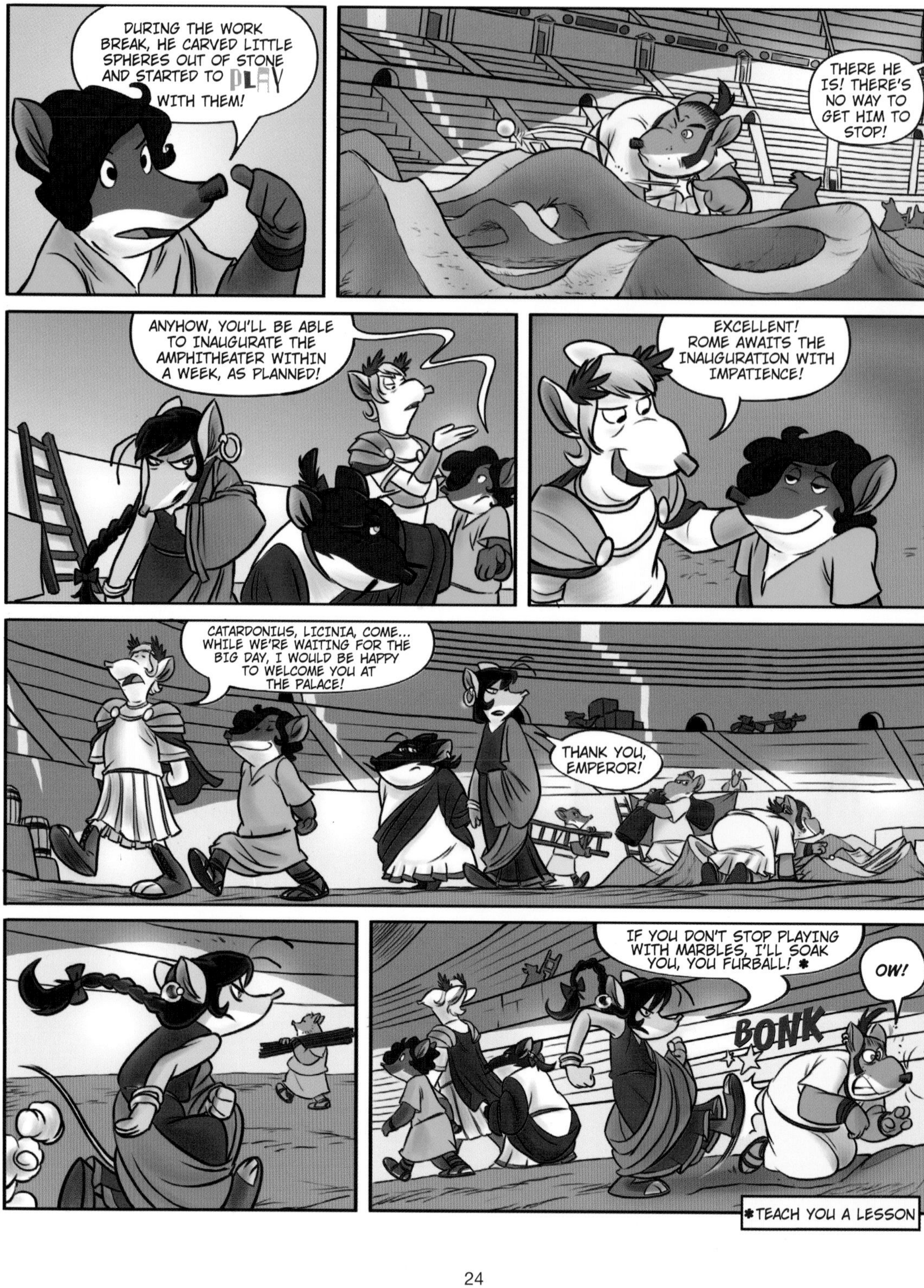
DURING THE WORK BREAK, HE CARVED LITTLE SPHERES OUT OF STONE AND STARTED TO PLAY WITH THEM!
THERE HE IS! THERE'S NO WAY TO GET HIM TO STOP!
ANYHOW, YOU'LL BE ABLE TO INAUGURATE THE AMPHITHEATER WITHIN A WEEK, AS PLANNED!
EXCELLENT! ROME AWAITS THE INAUGURATION WITH IMPATIENCE!
CATARDONIUS, LICINIA, COME... WHILE WE'RE WAITING FOR THE BIG DAY, I WOULD BE HAPPY TO WELCOME YOU AT THE PALACE!
THANK YOU, EMPEROR!
IF YOU DON'T STOP PLAYING WITH MARBLES, I'LL SOAK YOU, YOU FURBALL! ✱
OW!
BONK
✱TEACH YOU A LESSON

FINALLY, WE ALSO ARRIVED IN ANCIENT ROME...

A FEW MORE DRY BRANCHES AND THE SPEEDRAT WILL BE COMPLETELY CAMOU-FLAGED!

IS THIS BUSH OKAY, THEA?

LOOK OUT: THAT'S A NETTLE! AND TAKE THAT THING OFF YOUR HEAD. IN THIS PERIOD, THOSE HATS DIDN'T EVEN EXIST YET!

I'M KEEPING MY HAT: IT'S A PRESENT FROM MY GRANDMA. BUT IF YOU ASK ME TO DO IT...

HEE, HEE!

WELL DONE! AND NOW LET'S GET GOING! THE PIRATE CATS ALREADY HAVE ENOUGH OF A LEAD ON US!

TRACKING THEM DOWN IN A CITY AS BIG AS ROME ISN'T GOING TO BE EASY!

MAYBE IT WOULD BE BETTER TO SPLIT UP INTO TWO LITTLE GROUPS TO SEARCH!

RIGHT! YOU AND GERONIMO WILL GO TO THE COLISEUM: ITS INAUGURATION IS OUR ONLY TRAIL.

MEANWHILE THE KIDS AND I WILL SEARCH THE CITY!

25

SEE YOU THIS EVENING AT THE COLISEUM!

OKAY! CIAO!

SHE'S REALLY *pretty,* EH?

INDEED! SHE'S A FASCINATING CITY!

TEE, HEE, HEE...WHAT WERE YOU THINKING OF, STILTON-BABY? I WAS REFERRING TO THEA!

AH... CERTAINLY. MY SISTER IS REALLY A FASCINATING RODENT!

A HALF HOUR LATER, IN FRONT OF THE COLISEUM...

HOW CAN WE SEARCH WITHOUT BEING NOTICED?

WE CAN GET HIRED AS WORKERS AT THE AMPHITHEATER! IT'LL BE EASIER TO KEEP AN EYE ON THE SITUATION FROM THE INSIDE!

YOU'RE RIGHT! LET'S ASK THAT RODENT IF THERE ARE ANY JOBS!

HELLO, MY NAME IS STILTONIUS, GERONIMUS STILTONIUS, AND HE IS MY FRIEND HERCULIUS POIRATUS. WE'D LIKE...

IF YOU'RE LOOKING FOR WORK, I'M SORRY: WE'RE ALL FULL!

OH, NO! NOW WHAT?

LUCIUS, DID I HEAR RIGHT? THESE TWO ARE LOOKING FOR **WORK?**

YES, RATICUM!

YOU SEEM LIKE STRONG RODENTS! YOU'LL DO FINE!

COME WITH ME!

THANKS!

I'D LIKE YOU TO SUBSTITUTE FOR CAIUS BONZUS! INSTEAD OF WORKING, HE SPENDS THE DAY PLAYING WITH MARBLES!

?!?

I KNEW I'D PLAY WITH MARBLES!

27

JUST HAVE HIM TELL YOU WHAT HIS JOB WAS!

I DIDN'T KNOW THAT THE ANCIENT ROMANS USED TO PLAY WITH marbles!

WHO KNOWS?

UMM...AVE!

AVE!

!!!

AAAHHHHHHHH

WHAT GOT INTO HIM?

I DON'T KNOW. THAT RODENT IS VERY STRANGE!

STRANGE! IT'S AS IF...

HERCULE?

WHERE ARE YOU, HERCULE?

HEE, HEE, HEE!

!!!

MMF, MMF...G-G-GERONIMO STILTON! I HAVE TO WARN TERSILLA AND CATARDONE IMMEDIATELY!

28

MEANWHILE, THEA, BENJAMIN, AND PANDORA...

WHAT A LOT OF PEOPLE ARE HERE AT THE market!

ALL THIS WALKING AROUND HAS MADE ME AS HUNGRY AS A HOUSECAT!

ME, TOO!

WHAT DO YOU THINK ABOUT LUNCH IN A TAVERNA...HUH?

DO YOU SMELL THAT AROMA?

BLECH! IT SEEMS LIKE THE SMELL OF HERRINGS!

HERRINGS FROM THE GATTICO SEA, TO BE PRECISE! AND WHERE THERE'S THAT SMELL, THERE'S USUALLY A CAT!

STRANGE, I STARTED TO SMELL IT WHEN THAT MATRON PASSED NEAR ME!

I SUSPECT THAT...

MATRONS

IN ANCIENT ROME, LADIES WERE CALLED MATRONS. BY LAW, WOMEN WERE ECONOMICALLY DEPENDENT ON THEIR FATHERS, HUSBANDS, OR CLOSEST MALE RELATIVES. THEY HAD NO RIGHTS BUT WERE VERY WELL RESPECTED AND LISTENED TO WITHIN THE FAMILY.

MAYBE, ROME ISN'T AS BIG AS WE THOUGHT AFTER ALL. LET'S FOLLOW HER!

WE HAVE TO BE CAREFUL NOT TO BE NOTICED!

HEY, WHERE'D SHE DISAPPEAR TO?

?!?

HERE I AM!

SPRIZZ

WHAT A STINK! BUT...THAT'S NO LONGER THE SMELL FROM BEFORE...I FEEL LIKE I'M PASSING OUT...

KOFF
KOFF
KOFF

HEE, HEE, HEE...

IT WAS A GOOD IDEA TO BRING THIS POLECAT ESSENCE TO STUN THOSE SNOOPS WITH! I'M REALLY CURIOUS TO SEE WHO THEY ARE!

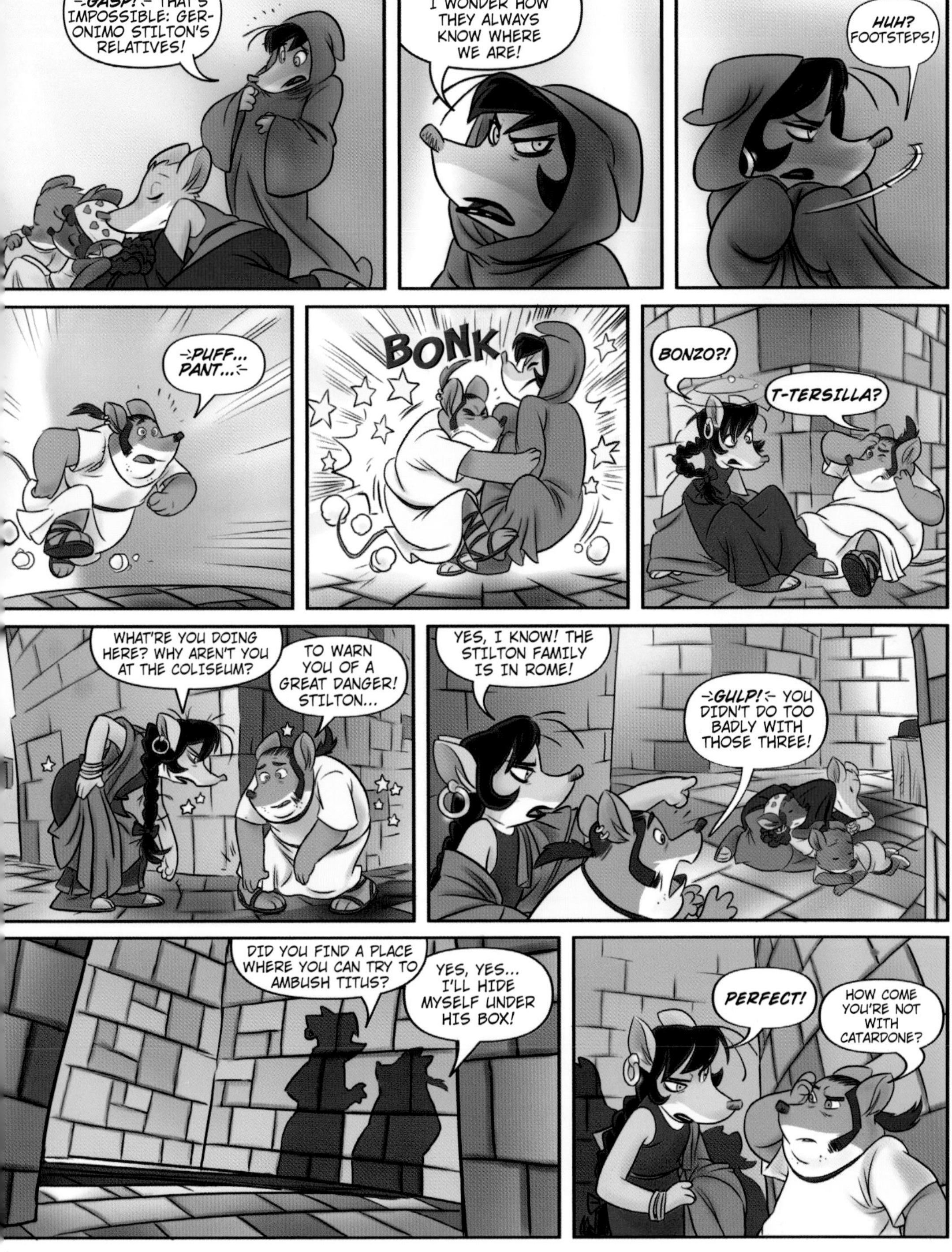
-GASP!- THAT'S IMPOSSIBLE: GERONIMO STILTON'S RELATIVES!
I WONDER HOW THEY ALWAYS KNOW WHERE WE ARE!
HUH? FOOTSTEPS!
-PUFF... PANT...-
BONK
BONZO?!
T-TERSILLA?
WHAT'RE YOU DOING HERE? WHY AREN'T YOU AT THE COLISEUM?
TO WARN YOU OF A GREAT DANGER! STILTON...
YES, I KNOW! THE STILTON FAMILY IS IN ROME!
-GULP!- YOU DIDN'T DO TOO BADLY WITH THOSE THREE!
DID YOU FIND A PLACE WHERE YOU CAN TRY TO AMBUSH TITUS?
YES, YES... I'LL HIDE MYSELF UNDER HIS BOX!
PERFECT!
HOW COME YOU'RE NOT WITH CATARDONE?

THEY WERE FILLING MY EARS* AT THE PALACE! CATARDONE AND TITUS WERE DOING NOTHING BUT REMINISCING...

*I WAS BORED

"...ABOUT THEIR YOUTHFUL HEROIC EXPLOITS!"

ONCE I ATTACKED A SHIP WITH A SUBMARINE!

A SUBMARINE? WHAT'S THAT?

WHAT SHOULD WE DO WITH THESE THREE RODENTS?

LOOK FOR SOME ROPE AND A BIGA. WE'LL TAKE THEM TO THE CATJET!

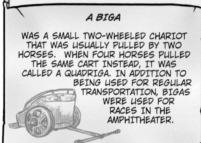

A BIGA

WAS A SMALL TWO-WHEELED CHARIOT THAT WAS USUALLY PULLED BY TWO HORSES. WHEN FOUR HORSES PULLED THE SAME CART INSTEAD, IT WAS CALLED A QUADRIGA. IN ADDITION TO BEING USED FOR REGULAR TRANSPORTATION, BIGAS WERE USED FOR RACES IN THE AMPHITHEATER.

HEE, HEE, HEE... THIS TIME I'VE GOT YOU IN THE PADS OF MY PAWS, GERONIMO STILTON!

THAT EVENING...

YOU'RE REALLY HOPELESS AT MARBLES! I WON EVERY TIME!

IT'S NOT MY FAULT THAT THE MARBLES WERE MADE OF STONE AND HURT MY FINGERS WHEN THEY HIT!

ACTUALLY, DIDN'T THAT CAIUS BONZUS' BEHAVIOR SEEM SUSPICIOUS TO YOU?

RIGHTRIGHTRIGHT...AS SOON AS HE SAW US, HE DASHED AWAY!

PERHAPS HE WAS ONE OF THE PIRATE CATS DRESSED AS A RODENT!

WHAT?!?

BUT...THEN, WE HAVE TO CHASE AFTER HIM!

WHY?

THE FACT THAT HE WAS HERE MEANS THE PIRATE CATS REALLY ARE AIMING FOR THE COLISEUM, SO THEY'LL BE BACK!

THINK SO?

YES, IF WE PRETEND WE DIDN'T RECOGNIZE HIM, HE'LL LEAD US TO HIS PALS IN DUE TIME!

THEA AND THE KIDS ARE LATE! I HOPE NOTHING'S HAPPENED TO THEM!

WHAT ARE YOU WORRIED ABOUT? YOUR SISTER HAS A BLACK BELT IN KARATE

I KNOW, BUT...

CLOMP CLOMP

SQUEAK!

!?

SWISH

WAK

!?

OUCH!

AND WHAT'S THIS?

BY THE FLEA-RIDDEN FUR OF A WERECAT!

33

HERCULE, LISTEN: "STILTON, YOUR SISTER AND THE KIDS ARE OUR PRISONERS! IF YOU WANT TO SEE THEM AGAIN SAFE AND SOUND, DON'T POKE YOUR NOSE INTO THE INAUGURATION OF THE COLISEUM! SIGNED: THE PIRATE CATS!"

BILLIONS OF BUNCHES OF BANANAS!

HURRY, STILTON-BABY, WE HAVE TO STOP THAT BIGA!

~PUFF~... IT'S GOING TOO FAST. WE'LL NEVER CATCH UP ON FOOT!

!

HOP ON BOARD, STILTON-BABY!

BUT...BUT... WE CAN'T STEAL IT!

WE'RE NOT STEALING IT; WE'RE JUST BORROWING IT... Y-YAAAHH!

MY BIGA! STOP, THIEF! STOP, THIEF!

HURRY, HERCULE!

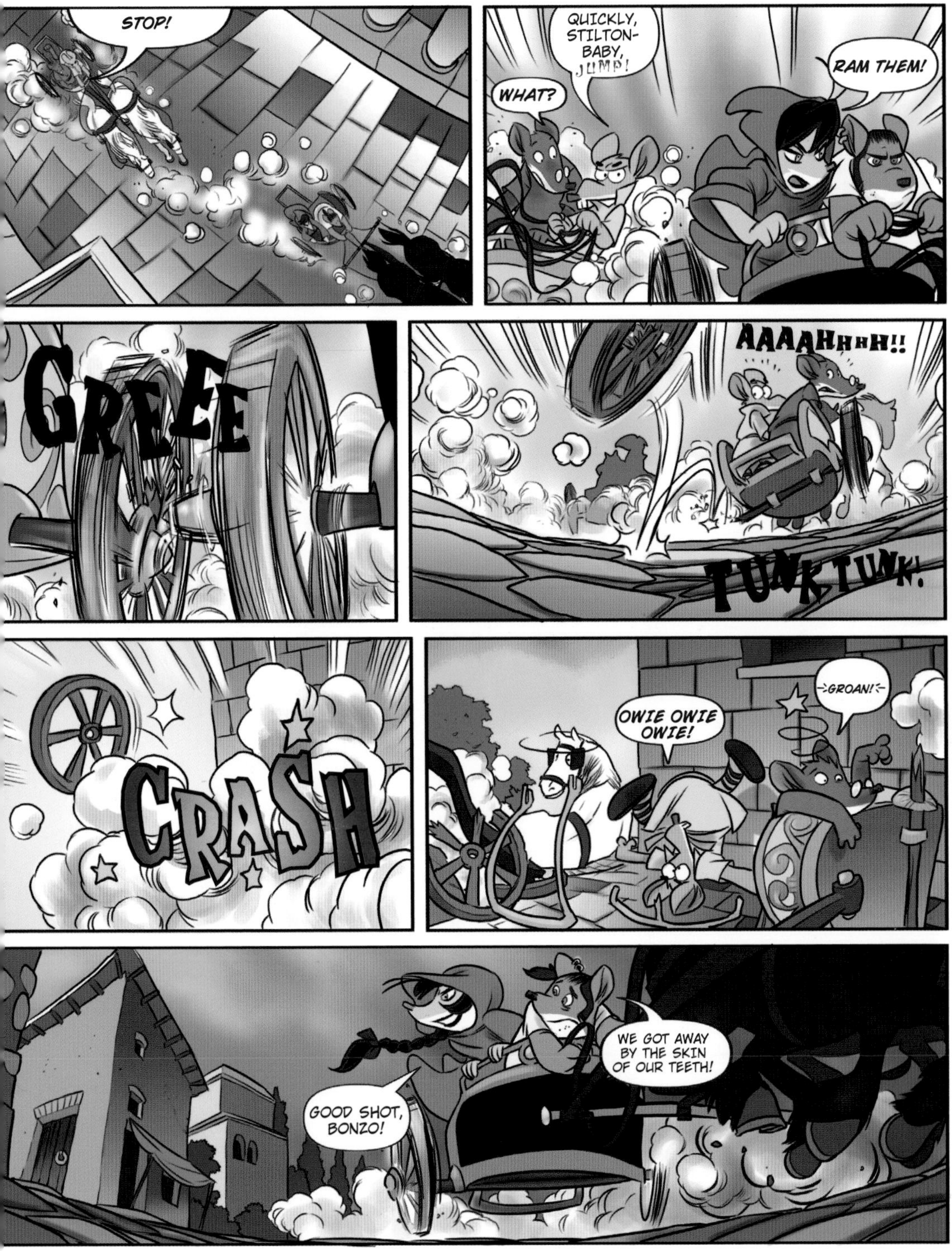
STOP!
QUICKLY, STILTON-BABY, JUMP!
WHAT?
RAM THEM!
GREEE
AAAAHHHH!!
TUNK TUNK!
CRASH
OWIE OWIE OWIE!
GROAN!
WE GOT AWAY BY THE SKIN OF OUR TEETH!
GOOD SHOT, BONZO!

THOSE RODENTS WON'T BE A PROBLEM ANY MORE!

EVERYTHING WHERE IT BELONGS, STILTON-BABY?

MOSTLY...

MY BIGA! MY BIGA!

UH-OH!

WE HAVE TO REPAY THAT RODENT FOR HIS BIGA!

LEAVE HIM A FEW SESTERCES, AND NOW... LET'S *SCRAM*

A LITTLE LATER, IN A TAVERNA...

-:SOB!:- HOW WILL WE GET BACK THEA, BENJAMIN, AND BUGSY?

TAVERNAS

IN ANCIENT ROME, THERE WERE MANY TAVERNAS, OFTEN LOCATED IN THE WORST AREAS OF THE CITY -- WHERE YOU COULD EAT DISHES WITH POLENTA, SPELT, BARLEY, AND VEGETABLES IN THEM. BESIDES THESE TAVERNS, THERE WERE ALSO THERMOPOLIAS, PLACES WHERE YOU COULD BUY HOT FOOD TO TAKE AWAY, LIKE MODERN TAKE-OUT FOOD.

DON'T CRY, STILTON-BABY!

EAT YOUR *CABBAGE* SOUP...

I'M NOT HUNGRY!

THIS SOUP MAY NOT BE VERY GOOD, BUT IF YOU WANT TO RESCUE THEA AND THE KIDS, YOU HAVE TO BE IN GOOD SHAPE!

RESCUE THEM? HOW? WE DON'T EVEN KNOW WHERE THE PIRATE CATS ARE HOLDING THEM PRISONER!

THAT'S TRUE, BUT IT'S CLEAR FROM THEIR LETTER THAT THOSE SCOUNDRELS INTEND TO MAKE THEIR MOVE ON THE DAY OF THE INAUGURATION!

IF WE'D ONLY MANAGED TO SEE THE FACES OF THOSE TWO IN THE BIGA, WE'D BE ABLE TO REC- OGNIZE THEM!

WE'VE STILL GOT CAIUS BONZUS!

GIVEN THAT HE'S REALLY A CAT, DO YOU THINK WE'LL SEE HIM AGAIN AT THE COLISEUM AFTER TONIGHT?

UMM... NO!

WE'RE UP A CREEK HUH?

I'M AFRAID SO!

MEANWHILE, AT THE IMPERIAL PALACE...

TERSILLA, WHERE DID YOU END UP? THE EMPEROR WAS WAITING FOR THE BANQUET!

CALL ME MOUSILLA, DADDY DEAR. SOMEONE MIGHT HEAR YOU!

IS EVERYTHING GOING WELL WITH TITUS?

OH, YES, WE'RE INSEPARABLE NOW!

THIS MORNING I EVEN GOT TO GO TO THE THERMAL BATHS WITH HIM... A TERRIBLE PLACE FOR A CAT!

THERMAL BATHS

IN ANCIENT ROME, THE THERMAL BATHS WERE PUBLIC BUILDINGS EQUIPPED WITH WASHROOMS, AND WERE ONE OF THE MAIN PLACES WHERE ALL CITIZENS COULD BE FOUND. BESIDES NUMEROUS POOLS FOR TAKING BATHS --WITH HOT, WARM, AND COLD WATER-- CHANGING ROOMS, SAUNAS, GYMS, AND, IN THE RICHER BATHS, EVEN THEATERS AND LIBRARIES.

"FIRST THEY TRIED TO BOIL ME IN A TYPE OF SAUNA...

...THEN I ALMOST *DROWNED* IN A POOL FULL OF WATER..."

...AND FINALLY A MASSEUR TRIED TO **DESTROY** MY BACK!"

I WAS SUCH A DEAD WEIGHT THEY HAD TO LOAD ME ONTO A SEDAN-CHAIR TO GO BACK TO THE PALACE!

TSK...DID ANYTHING ELSE HAPPEN?

AH, YES, I ALMOST FORGOT ABOUT THIS. TITUS PROPOSED THAT I BECOME A SENATOR!

SENATOR? BUT THAT'S A VERY IMPORTANT OFFICE!!!

THE SENATE
WAS THE MOST IMPORTANT ASSEMBLY IN ANCIENT ROME. THE TERM, SENATE, COMES FROM THE LATIN WORD, "SENEX," WHICH MEANS "OLD." AS A MATTER OF FACT, IT WAS RECOGNIZED THAT OLD PEOPLE HAD THE EXPERIENCE NEEDED TO MAKE IMPORTANT DECISIONS. FOR THIS REASON, THEREFORE, TO BECOME A SENATOR, BESIDES BEING OF NOBLE ORIGINS, A PERSON HAD TO BE OVER 43.

YOU DID A GOOD JOB, DADDY DEAR! LISTEN, I ALSO HAVE SOME NEWS...

BRIEFLY...

AREN'T YOU AFRAID THAT STILTON WILL BE ABLE TO HINDER MY...UM, OUR... PLAN?

NO, HE WON'T DARE COME NEAR THE COLISEUM AS LONG AS WE HAVE HIS FRIENDS AS HOSTAGES!

FOR SECURITY, I'VE ORDERED BONZO TO STAND GUARD ON THE CATJET!

BUT...I THOUGHT HE WAS GOING TO BE WORKING INSIDE THE AMPHITHE-ATER.

IT'S BETTER IF HE STAYS HIDDEN FOR NOW: STILTON WOULD BE ABLE TO RECOG-NIZE HIM! HE'LL COME FOR THE INAUGURATION OF THE COLISEUM!

I HOPE HE DOESN'T MESS UP AT THE CATJET!

COME ON, DADDY DEAR! HE WON'T BE ABLE TO DO THAT...

"...HE JUST HAS TO KEEP HIS EYES OPEN!"

ZZZZZ

ZZZZZ

THE FOLLOWING DAY, HERCULE AND I MOVED AROUND IN ROME, UNDECIDED ABOUT WHAT TO DO...

WE ABSOLUTELY HAVE TO FIND A WAY TO RESCUE THEA AND THE KIDS...

AND FOIL THE PIRATE CATS' PLAN.

RIGHT!

BILLIONS OF BUNCHES OF BANANAS! DID YOU SEE HOW MANY RODENTS ARE IN FRONT OF THE COLISEUM?

THEY'RE ALL HERE FOR THE INAUGURATION! WHAT A MESS!

WE HAVE TO COME UP WITH AN IDEA!

MAYBE WE CAN TRY TO TRAP THE PIRATE CATS IN FRONT OF THE AMPHITHEATER...

AND FORCE THEM TO SHOW US WHERE OUR FRIENDS ARE!

HMM...

REMEMBER THEY'RE WEARING MOUSE MASKS! IT'LL BE HARD TO RECOGNIZE THEM!

STILTONIUS SQUEAKIUS, WHAT A PLEASURE TO SEE YOU!

UMMM... AVE, ARCHITECT RATICUM!

AVE!

DID YOU COME FOR THE INAUGURATION, TOO?

WELL, HERE'S...

AND CAIUS BONZUS? HAVE YOU NEWS OF HIM, BY CHANCE? I HAVEN'T SEEN HIM SINCE YESTERDAY!

TO TELL THE TRUTH...

POOR GUY, I HOPE HE DIDN'T GET SICK...HE SAID HE LIVED AT THE CLOACA MAXIMA...AND IT'S CERTAINLY NOT A VERY HEALTHY PLACE TO LIVE...

!?

!?

BONZUS LIVES IN THE CLOACA **MAXIMA?!?**

YES, THAT'S THE ADDRESS HE GAVE WHEN HE WAS HIRED!

HE'S REALLY A BIZARRE GUY, ACTUALLY MOUSE! OUT OF MANY PLACES, HE PICKED THE MOST...

BUT... WHERE DID THEY GO?

RUN, STILTON-BABY! RUN!

IN THE MEANTIME, AT THE PALACE...

ONLY A FEW MORE HOURS UNTIL THE COLISEUM WILL BE MINE!

OURS, DADDY DEAR, OURS!

WHEN BONZO PRETENDS TO ATTACK THE EMPEROR, I SUGGEST YOU BE THE FIRST TO SPRING TO HIS DEFENSE!

I'LL BE THE SPRINGIEST! BONZO WON'T GET AWAY!

DON'T HURT HIM; JUST MAKE HIM RUN AWAY!

OOF! NOT EVEN A KICK TO THE END OF HIS TAIL!

NOT EVEN THAT!

FINALLY WE ARRIVED AT THE CLOACA MAXIMA.

THIS WAY!

BRRR...THIS DARK SEWER GIVES ME THE JITTERS...

TO SAY NOTHING OF THE *STINK* HERE!

LOOK OVER THERE, STILTON-BABY!

THAT MUST BE THE PIRATE CATS' TIME MACHINE! YOU WERE RIGHT TO SUSPECT CAIUS BONZUS!

WE HAVE TO BE QUIET!

I'LL BE AS QUIET AS A MOUSE!

LUCKILY THERE DOESN'T SEEM TO BE ANYONE IN THE NEIGHBORHOOD!

BONK

!

THEA?!?

HERCULE?!?

UNCLE GERONIMO?

UH?

BENJAMIN, I'M SO HAPPY TO SEE YOU AGAIN!

ME, TOO, UNCLE GERONIMO!

SORRY ABOUT HITTING YOU, LITTLE BROTHER. I WAS AFRAID YOU WERE THE PIRATE CATS!

IT DOESN'T MATTER! THE IMPORTANT THING IS THAT YOU'RE SAFE AND SOUND!

TELL ME, BUGSY-BABY, HOW DID YOU GET YOURSELVES FREE?

THEA DESERVES THE CREDIT! SHE UNTIED OUR ROPES AND PUT THAT CHEESEHEAD WATCHING US OUT OF ACTION.

IT WASN'T HARD: HE WAS ASLEEP!

AND WHERE'S HE NOW?

HERE!

MMMM!

THERE'S NOT A MINUTE TO LOSE! WE'VE GOT TO GO TO THE COLISEUM! THE OTHER PIRATE CATS WILL BE READY TO STRIKE!

FIRST, LET'S QUESTION THIS SCOUNDREL TO FIND OUT THEIR PLAN!

I ALREADY DID THAT! I QUESTIONED HIM WHEN I WAS TYING HIM UP!

THEA QUICKLY BROUGHT US UP TO SPEED ABOUT EVERYTHING...

WITHOUT THEIR ACCOMPLICE, TERSILLA AND CATARDONE CAN'T PUT THEIR PLAN INTO ACTION...

RIGHT, BUT WE'D BETTER NOT RELY ON THAT: TERSILLA COULD MAKE UP ANOTHER PLAN ON THE SPOT! WE'D BETTER GO TO THE COLISEUM, ANYHOW, AND UNMASK THEM!

AND WHAT SHOULD WE DO WITH BONZO?

I'D SAY WE SHOULD LEAVE HIM HERE!

YES, BUT FIRST I WANT TO CHECK HOW...

>SQUEAK!<

HURRY UP! WE HAVE TO STOP HIM BEFORE HE MANAGES TO GET FREE!

GET GOING, STILTON-BABY!

NNNGG!

MEANWHILE, AT THE COLISEUM, EVERYONE WAS WAITING FOR THE ENTRANCE OF THE EMPEROR, SO THAT THE HUNDRED DAYS OF SPECTACLES THAT HAD BEEN ANNOUNCED TO CELEBRATE ITS CONSTRUCTION COULD GET UNDERWAY...

TITUS!
TITUS!
TITUS!
TITUS!
TITUS!
TITUS!
TITUS!
TITUS!
TITUS!
TITUS!

THE INAUGURATION OF THE COLISEUM

WAS A MEMORABLE EVENT IN ROMAN HISTORY. IN FACT, TITUS ORDERED IT TO BE CELEBRATED BY A HUNDRED DAYS OF SPECTACLES, WHICH ENTERTAINED THE PUBLIC FROM MORNING UNTIL EVENING. THE EMPEROR NOT ONLY WANTED TO GIVE HIS FAMILY'S NAME PRESTIGE, BUT ALSO TO WIN THE PEOPLE'S AFFECTION.

THIS DAY WILL GO DOWN IN HISTORY!

YOU'RE RIGHT, DEAR TITUS, BUT NOT IN THE WAY YOU THINK!

GET READY TO SPRING TO THE EMPEROR'S DEFENSE!

I'LL BE THE SPRINGIEST!

LET'S HOPE THAT BONZO GETS HERE IN TIME AND THAT THERE'S NO MORE NEWS SINCE YESTER-DAY...

SPRINGIEST! SPRINGIEST!

MEANWHILE, BONZO...

~PUFF, PANT!~

~PUFF!~

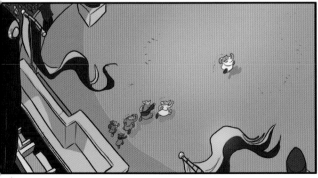

LOOK! BONZO'S CLIMBING ON THE PLATFORMS!

HERE'S THE ENTRANCE TO MY **BOX**!

-)MMF...
MMF...(-

!?

THE...S-S-STI...MMF...

RATICUM, WHAT'S THIS WORKER DOING HERE?

I DON'T KNOW...

WHY IS THAT DUMMY STILL WEARING HIS MOUSE MASK?

CHAAAAAARGE!

NO, WAIT!

!?

CRASH

GLUB!

WHAT A DUMMY!

WHY DID YOUR FATHER JUMP LIKE THAT?

EVERYTHING'S SO STRANGE...

UMM...MAY I COME IN?

?!?

WELL, RATICUM! COULD YOU TELL ME WHAT ALL THESE RODENTS ARE DOING HERE?

TRULY, I...

~GULP!~ GERONIMO STILTON?!?

UH-OH!

FORGIVE THE INTRUSION, EMPEROR... BUT I MUST UNMASK THESE SCOUNDRELS!

MEOW!

BY JUPITER'S BEARD! CATARDONIUS IS..IS...A CAT?!

HOW IS THAT POSSIBLE?!?

HIS DAUGHTER MOUSILLA AND CAIUS BONZUS ARE TOO!

GRRR... YOU'RE NOT GOING TO GET US SO EASILY!

THEY'RE ESCAPING!

THUD!

MIAOOWWW!

SBAM

INCREDIBLE! THEY MANAGED TO GET AWAY AGAIN!

THEY ESCAPED RIGHT OUT FROM UNDER OUR NOSES!

VICTORY IS YOURS, STILTON! BUT SOONER OR LATER WE'LL MEET AGAIN!

SO HERE WE ARE AT THE END OF OUR ADVENTURE. ONCE AGAIN, WE'D PREVENTED THE PIRATE CATS FROM CHANGING HISTORY!

IT'S ALL YOUR FAULT, BONZO! IF I CATCH YOU, I'M GOING TO REDRAW THE SPOTS ON YOUR FUR!*

BUT, TERSILLA... I...

*TEACH YOU A LESSON!

LEAVING OUT THE DETAILS OF OUR TRIP THROUGH TIME, I TOLD THE EMPEROR THE WHOLE TRUTH ABOUT THE NEFARIOUS INTENTIONS OF CATARDONIUS, MOUSILLA, AND CAIUS BONZUS!

AND THAT'S THE STORY!

WHAT SCOUNDRELS!

THE EMPEROR WAS SO TAKEN BY OUR COURAGE THAT HE INVITED US TO WATCH THE INAUGURATION OF THE COLISEUM FROM HIS BOX...

48

..AND THAT EVENING HE WANTED US TO BE THE GUESTS OF HONOR AT A GRAND BANQUET!

THE NEXT DAY, WE SAID GOODBYE TO OUR NEW FRIEND. AFTER SO MUCH DANGER...

FAREWELL, FRIENDS!

...WE COULDN'T WAIT TO GET BACK HOME!

THERE YOU ARE!

Geronimo!

PROFESSOR VOLT!

COME ON, TELL ME EVERYTHING!

YOU'RE NOT GOING TO BELIEVE YOUR EARS!

A LITTLE LATER...

HMMM... WHO KNOWS IF TITUS WOULD HAVE GRANTED THE PIRATE CATS' WISH TO NAME THE AMPHITHEATER AFTER CATARDONIUS...

LUCKILY, WE'LL NEVER KNOW!

ANYWAY, I'M SURE THOSE CHEESEHEADS WILL BE AT IT AGAIN VERY SOON!

RIGHT!

BY THE WAY, THERE COULD BE ANOTHER MISSION I WANT TO ENTRUST YOU WITH!

ANOTHER?

BUT WE JUST GOT BACK!

OH, NO, SORRY, YOU MISUNDER-STOOD ME. IT'S NOT ABOUT THE PIRATE CATS...EVEN THOUGH I MUST ADMIT IT'S A RATHER DELICATE TASK!

COME ON, PROFESSOR! DON'T KEEP US ON TENTERHOOKS!

I IMPLORE YOU: YOU ABSOLUTELY HAVE TO SAVE MY REFRIGERATOR FROM YOUR COUSIN! HE ARRIVED HERE AS SOON AS YOU LEFT... AND HE'S DONE NOTHING BUT EAT!

TRAP?

~BURP!~ WELCOME BACK, COUSINS! DOES ANYONE HAPPEN TO HAVE AN AFTER-DINNER MINT?

MY DEAR RODENT FRIENDS, FAREWELL UNTIL THE NEXT ADVENTURE...ANOTHER WHISKERFUL OF AN ADVENTURE, WRITTEN BY STILTON...

Geronimo Stilton!

WATCH OUT FOR PAPERCUTZ

Howdy! It's me Jim Salicrup, the ancient Editor-in-Chief of Papercutz, the publishers of the GERONIMO STILTON graphic novels – not to mention the BIONICLE, CLASSICS ILLUSTRATED, DISNEY FAIRIES (coming soon!), HARDY BOYS, NANCY DREW, and TALES FROM THE CRYPT too. But of course, you probably already know all that, especially if you're a regular visitor to www.papercutz.com and follower of the world-famous Papercutz Blog!

Like I said in the "WATCH OUT FOR PAPERCUTZ" page in GERONIMO STILTON Graphic Novel #2 "The Secret of the Sphinx," although both Geronimo Stilton and I are both Editors-in-Chief, Geronimo can travel through time, but I can't! But, believe it or not, I've been working on that. Even now, as I type these words in your past, I'm communicating with you in my future! I admit, that's not nearly as impressive as my actually traveling through time, but it's a start!

Another way I've discovered to kinda travel through time is by the pages of this graphic novel. At any point in "The Coliseum Con" I can either go forward or back in time in the story by simply flipping the pages ahead or back. Again, I admit that's not as impressive as what Geronimo can do in his Speedrat, but hey, I don't have Professor Volt helping me out here!

Finally, for a real peek at the future, simply turn this page and check out the preview of GERONIMO STILTON Graphic Novel #4 "Following the Trail of Marco Polo!" Now, if you're picking up this graphic novel soon after it went on sale in bookstores everywhere, then you'll have to wait until April of 2010 for the rest of the Marco Polo story! Think about it! You have to wait until the future before you can go way back into the past again with Geronimo! But if you picked up this graphic novel anytime after April 2010, you may have already read "Following the Trail of Marco Polo" and are picking up this graphic novel because somehow you might've missed it when it first came out!

Enough! Time travel makes my head spin! The best way to find out what's going on right now—in your present time—is to check us out on www.papercutz.com! See you there!

Thanks,

Jim

Caricature drawn by Steve Brodner at the MoCCA Art Fest.

Special Preview of GERONIMO STILTON Graphic Novel #4 – "Following the Trail of Marco Polo"

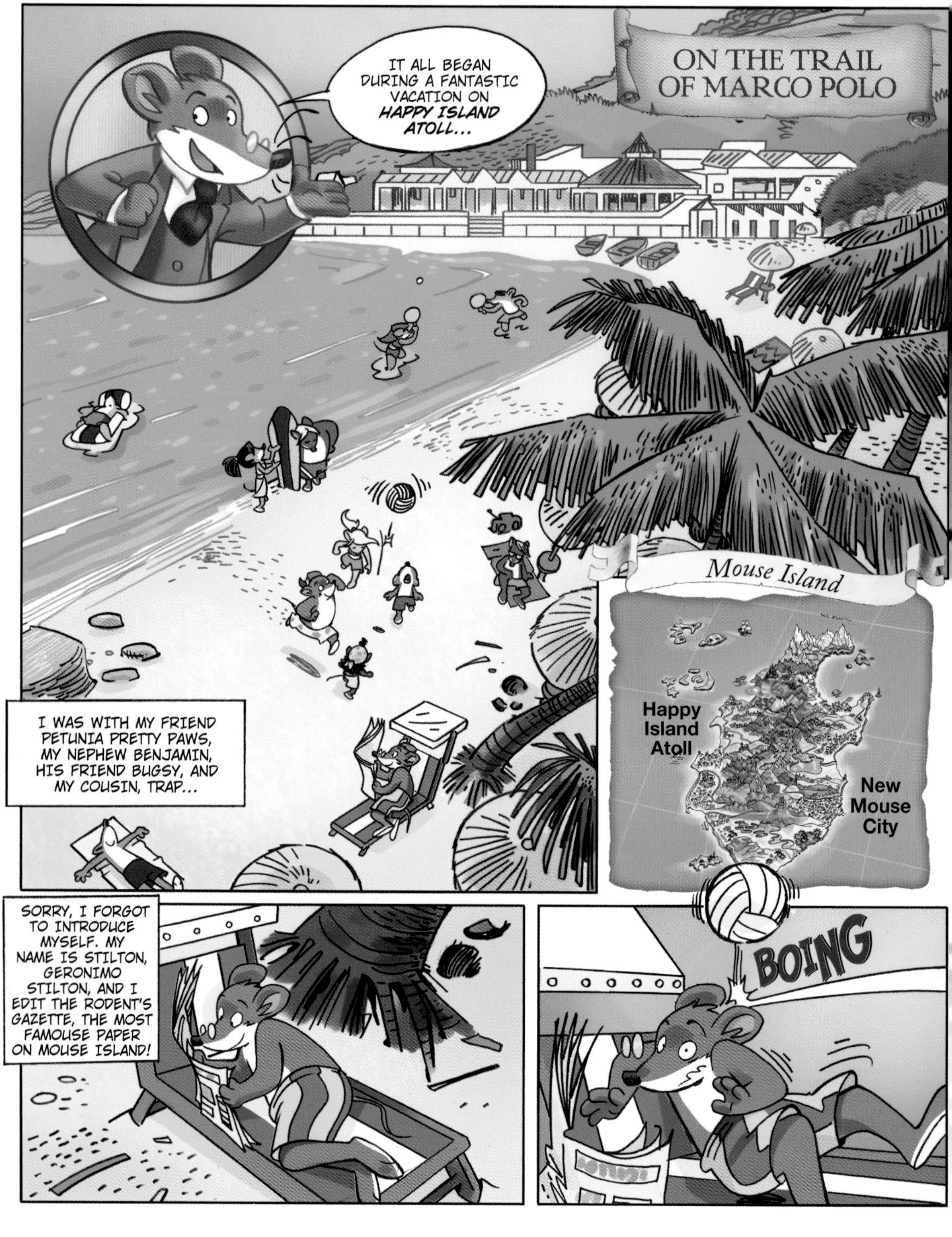
IT ALL BEGAN DURING A FANTASTIC VACATION ON *HAPPY ISLAND ATOLL*...
ON THE TRAIL OF MARCO POLO
I WAS WITH MY FRIEND PETUNIA PRETTY PAWS, MY NEPHEW BENJAMIN, HIS FRIEND BUGSY, AND MY COUSIN, TRAP...
Mouse Island
Happy Island Atoll
New Mouse City
SORRY, I FORGOT TO INTRODUCE MYSELF. MY NAME IS STILTON, GERONIMO STILTON, AND I EDIT THE RODENT'S GAZETTE, THE MOST FAMOUSE PAPER ON MOUSE ISLAND!
BOING

...THEN, I WAS BLASTED BY A SANDSTORM...

I WAS ON VACATION, BUT I WASN'T RESTING VERY MUCH. AFTER I GOT HIT BY A BALL, A CRAB PINCHED ME...

...AND LAST OF ALL, I WAS MISTAKEN FOR A **FISH** BY A FLOCK OF SEAGULLS!

TO HELP ME RELAX, TRAP PERSUADED ME TO GO WATERSKIING...

STAND UP AS SOON THE SPEEDBOAT TAKES OFF!

UHM... I'LL TRY!

MAYBE IT WOULD'VE BEEN EASIER IF YOU'D PUT SKIS ON ME INSTEAD OF THESE THINGS!

TRUST ME, DEAR COUSIN. THOSE THINGS ARE THE AQUATIC VERSION OF **SNOW.**

MAYBE SO... BUT THEY SEEM LIKE TOTALLY NORMAL BEACH TENNIS PADDLES!

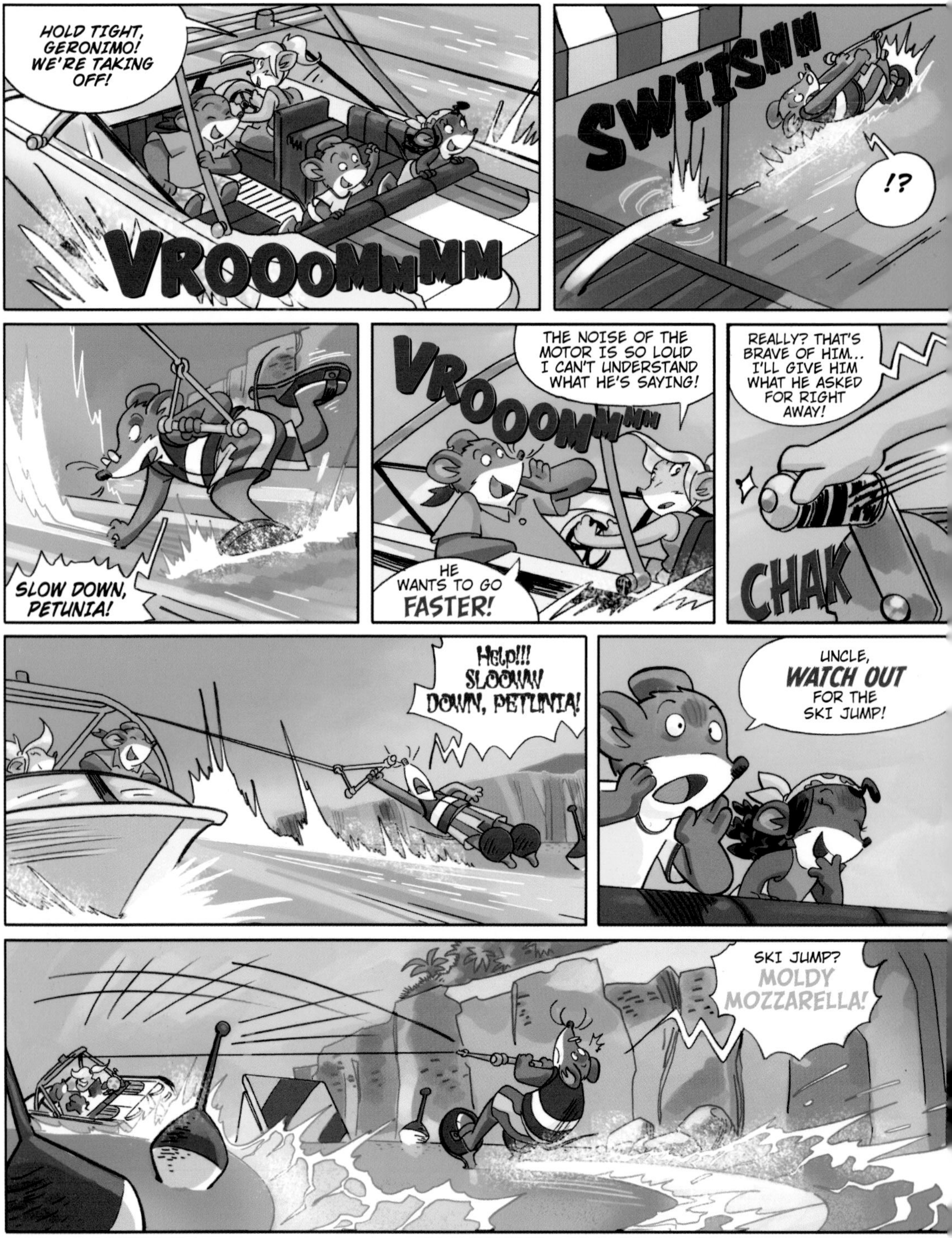
HOLD TIGHT, GERONIMO! WE'RE TAKING OFF!
VROOOMMMM
SWISHH
!?
SLOW DOWN, PETUNIA!
VROOOMMMM
THE NOISE OF THE MOTOR IS SO LOUD I CAN'T UNDERSTAND WHAT HE'S SAYING!
HE WANTS TO GO FASTER!
REALLY? THAT'S BRAVE OF HIM... I'LL GIVE HIM WHAT HE ASKED FOR RIGHT AWAY!
CHAK
Help!!! SLOOWW DOWN, PETUNIA!
UNCLE, WATCH OUT FOR THE SKI JUMP!
SKI JUMP? MOLDY MOZZARELLA!

AAAH!

SPLASH

Rollicking rats!
AMAZING! I'M STILL ALL IN ONE PIECE!

HEY, DID YOU SEE UNCLE GERONIMO'S FANTASTIC JUMP?

I'D BETTER SLOW DOWN! I WOULDN'T WANT HIM TO HURT HIMSELF!

NO, PETUNIA, YOU WORRY TOO MUCH! GERONIMO'S HAVING SO MUCH **FUN...**

"...WHAT COULD POSSIBLY HAPPEN TO HIM IN THE MIDDLE OF THEOCEAN?"

CRUNCH

HUH?

WHAT'S GOING ON?

~GULP!~

HEEEELP! A SHARK'S CHASING ME!!!

WHAT'S HE *YELLING* ABOUT NOW?

DON'T WORRY ABOUT IT. HE ALWAYS DOES THAT... HE'S A FRAIDY-MOUSE!

WIRRR

QUICK, AUNT PETUNIA, HEAD FOR THE SHORE: GERONIMO'S BEING FOLLOWED BY A SHARK!

WHAT?!?

~SQUEEEAK!~

WHUMP

HE FELL INTO THE *WATER!* WE'VE GOT TO GET HIM OUT RIGHT NOW!

WSSSHHH

Don't miss GERONIMO STILTON
Graphic Novel #4 – "Following the Trail of Marco Polo"